Richard Scarry's
NAUGHTY BUNNY

A GOLDEN BOOK • NEW YORK
Western Publishing Company, Inc., Racine, Wisconsin 53404

The little bunny didn't mean to be naughty.
But he didn't try very hard to be good.
He bothered his father at breakfast.
He spilled his cereal and his milk.

The bunny's daddy said, "If you
will try to be a good little bunny,
I will bring you home a present
from the city."
The little bunny promised to try.

Mrs. Bunny turned on the television to little bunny's favorite program.

The little bunny turned the sound up loud and nearly frightened his mother out of her wits.

Oh, naughty bunny.

Mrs. Bunny gave him some crayons and a coloring book.
Look what he did.
Oh, naughty bunny.
The naughty bunny was sent to his room.
Poor little bunny.

Soon Mrs. Bunny looked in to see if he was being good.
What a mess the bunny made of his room!
His dear sweet mother was exasperated.
She sent the bunny outside to play.

William, who was the bunny's
best friend, came over to play.
They leaped, and they ran.

They kicked.

The little bunny picked some flowers.

William ran quickly to tell the little bunny's mother.

At first Mrs. Bunny was furious.
But she just couldn't scold the little bunny,
because he had picked them for her.

The little bunny pushed William for being a tattletale.

William fell into a mud puddle.
Kersplash!

William went home crying.

William's mother telephoned the little bunny's mother.

Oh, why couldn't her little bunny be a nice little bunny like William?

Mrs. Bunny had to call the little bunny twelve times to come to lunch.
He finally came.

He didn't want an egg sandwich.
He wanted peanut butter.
He wouldn't finish his milk.
He ate only half of his sandwich.

He made a fuss at naptime.
Oh, naughty bunny.

The little bunny didn't nap…

until he heard his mother coming.

"Oh, what a dear, darling bunny he is when he is asleep," she thought.

After his nap the little bunny's mother sent him out to play.

He chased a fly in his father's workshop.

He visited the chickens in the barnyard, and he left
the gate open behind him.

Oh, naughty bunny.

When his father came home, he asked, "Has he been a good little bunny?"

His mother answered, "Well, he tried to be a good little bunny, but sometimes he forgot."

Daddy gave the little bunny a present for trying to be good.

They sat down to supper.

The little bunny kissed his mother good night, and his daddy gave him a piggyback to bed.

Instead of going right to sleep, the little bunny wanted a glass of water.

He wanted to go to the bathroom.

His mother went into his room to make him go to sleep.
She told him that it made her very sad when he was naughty.
The little bunny loved his mother dearly and didn't like
to see her sad.
He told her that tomorrow he was definitely going to be a
good little bunny.

And the next day the little bunny
was a very good bunny, indeed!
He didn't bother Daddy at breakfast.
He didn't spill his cereal.

He ate all his lunch.

He had his nap
without a fuss.

He played nicely with William.

He was so good, his mother didn't have to send him to his room, not once.

It was such fun to be good.

And then, after supper...

the little bunny painted a picture of himself.
   It was a present for his mother.
   His mother was very pleased.
   She hugged him and kissed him, and she tucked him into bed.
And she said, "Oh, how I love my naughty little angel."